WHAT THE SEA WANTS

LizStar
BOOKS

White Hall, Maryland

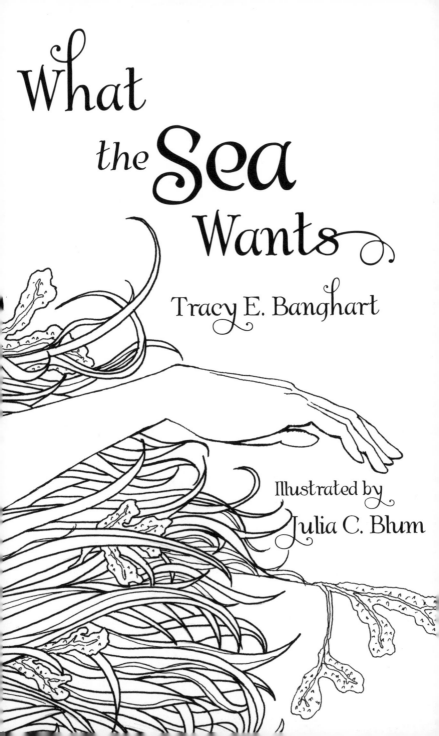

What the Sea Wants

Tracy E. Banghart

Illustrated by
Julia C. Blum

www.lizstarbooks.com

Book design by Tracy E. Banghart and Julia C. Blum
Printed in the United Kingdom by Biddles Ltd.

ISBN-13: 978-0-9779753-0-3
ISBN-10: 0-9779753-0-4

10 9 8 7 6 5 4 3 2

*To all the wise women in my life, especially
my grandmother, Elizabeth Raynes Banghart,
who introduced me to the magic of Maine.*

~T.E.B.

*For my grandparents, D.M.B. & M.S.B., and the ship-shaped
house that introduced me to the ocean and for my grandmother,
M.A.B.C., captain's daughter and lifelong adventurer, in fond
memory of the seas we sailed together.*

~J.C.B.

1

The day the sea took Victoria, the fog rode the ocean so low there was no horizon, only a wall of murky gray. A cove like a broken bowl pushed against the fog, its jagged evergreen edges piercing the barrier while the ocean flowed through the gap and into shore. The tide was high and on its way out, and the dregs left above the water line were gooey and dangerously slick. Standing as sentinels along the water, boulders protected tide pools and seaweed beds. Three seagulls dove, crying, through pale, soupy currents of air.

Victoria stood watching the gulls, her slight figure blurry and insubstantial in the fog. Her pale skin glowed in the bluish predawn light, and her deep-set, aquamarine eyes crinkled at the corners as she stared into the mist, as if by concentrating she could see through its boundaries out to sea. Dark hair tangled down her back like matted seaweed, curly and stiff with sea spray. Hovering at the edge of the beach, under the protection of the evergreens, she blended so perfectly with the wild mass of forest just behind her that it was difficult to tell whether she stood there at all.

Victoria Winslow lived with her mother and Grannie Foster up the hill from the cove, in a small clapboard cottage with a porch that ran the length of the house and a garden where Victoria's mother grew vegetables and herbs. Like Victoria, the house was small and insubstantial looking, hidden from the road by shade trees and lupine. Rose vines curled insistent green tendrils among twisted raspberry bushes and through the porch railings, so that pink and white blossoms nodded onto the porch and dropped blowsy petals onto the salt-eroded wood. Huge bushes of lupine grew in sprays of pink and purple next to the house where the old climbing tree bent against the endless bullying of the ocean wind. Sometimes Victoria would stand on the porch, hands on the rail between rose and raspberry thorns, and stare down the sloping grassy hill that led to the ocean, but she spent most of her time on the rocky beach, closer to the sea.

Everyday, Victoria would wander down along the shore, collecting things and singing to herself. She knew the tides and the winds that blew through the cove and coaxed the fog out to sea. Watching for seals out in the harbor, she would sometimes even see the pearly scales of a mermaid's tail catch the sunlight and glitter at the far end of the cove. She found old buoys, perfect skipping stones, and driftwood in exotic and twisted shapes that reminded her of her grandmother's stories.

The story Victoria asked to hear most often was the one about the Captain. "My dear girl," Grannie Foster would begin, her voice pitched low and her eyes narrowed as if she told some great secret, "The world is full of many mysteries. Miracles, tragedies. Things that neither you nor I can explain. The sea holds the power to bring about these mysteries." Here Grannie Foster smiled and her eyes softened at the corners, "The sea *is* the mystery," she whispered. Victoria nodded sagely, as if this made perfect sense to her.

"But Grannie, what about the Captain?" she asked.

"Oh, yes. Let's see," Grannie Foster said. "There once was an old sea captain who lived in the cabin down on the beach, in our little bay. His name was John Westcott, and he was the captain of a schooner named the Waverly. Most folks just called him Captain."

Here Grannie Foster leaned back in her chair and paused, and Victoria asked on cue, "Was the Waverly a nice boat?"

"Ship, dear. Ship," Grannie reminded gently. "Oh, she was bonnie to be sure, with two white sails and a shiny clean deck. The Waverly was the Captain's pride. Until one night, when the poor ship met a terrible fate."

"What happened, Grannie?" Victoria queried.

"Well, no one really knows. The Captain sailed her from Maine to Massachusetts. A lumber trader he was, or so the story goes. Folks said he was an honest man, but back in those days there were a lot of dark goings on, so you never could tell." Every once in a while, Victoria would ask about these dark deeds, but Grannie would just smile a sad half-smile and continue with the story. "One night, a storm struck off the coast as the Captain was sailing up from Boston. A thick fog hid the dangerous shoals to the south, and the Waverly ran aground. The crew perished in the sea. Back then, it was considered bad luck for a man to be rescued from drowning, so even though some folks saw what was happening, no one came to the sailors' aid."

"Why? Why was it bad luck?"

"Well, I'll tell you, honey. No one wanted to anger the sea. If a ship went down or a man went overboard, people just thought of that as the sea's will and wouldn't interfere, in case the sea took vengeance for that person's meddling. You don't want to meddle with the sea, Victoria. Superstitions are just superstitions, but every rumor, every legend starts with a grain of truth. No need to tempt fate, as they say." Here she would pat Victoria's hand and the girl knew she was thinking about Victoria's father.

"What happened to the Captain, Grannie? Did he drown too?"

"No, he did not. The captain is meant to stay aboard to ensure the safety of his men—or his cargo—but somehow John Westcott survived, though his men and cargo did not. No one knew how, but everybody had a theory. Some folks said the sea saw that he was a good man and had mercy on him. Others said it knew the truth, that his heart was as black as rot, and so it threw him to shore in disgust. And still others swore that his mistress, a quiet widow with long wild hair like yours, saw him in the flotsam of the murdered boat and saved him." Grannie Foster leaned forward and whispered conspiratorially, "Some say they saw her walking into the water, lit by flashes of lightning, and then she just disappeared. And when morning came the Captain was sprawled on the beach, and his mistress, the Lady Elizabeth, was gone, never to be found.

"Because you see, Victoria, if Lady Elizabeth saved her love, the sea would demand a price. A life for a life, as they say." Here Victoria shivered and imagined the fair Lady Elizabeth, giving her life to save the handsome Captain.

"The Captain," Grannie Foster continued, "never recovered from the loss of the Waverly, or perhaps it was the loss of Lady Elizabeth. We will never know. He spent the rest of his life keeping watch over the sea, maybe hoping it would return his love to him. He lived in the cottage on the bay and passed each day and night on his porch, rocking in a chair as old and creaky as he was." Grannie sipped her tea and let a moment or two pass before saying, "Anytime someone would walk along the shore in front of his house, he would call down to them in a quavering, rusty voice," She lowered her voice and added a scratchy undertone, " 'You there! Did you hear the storm last night? Did you hear the voices in the rain?' or he'd call out a warning, 'Don't walk too near the water, boy. The sea's in a fine mood today and she'll eat you for breakfast if you let her.' He told of strange things he'd seen during the violent storms that pushed in from the ocean, of lightning revealing dark, twisted creatures on the beach at low tide. No one would meet his piercing eyes and the villagers kept their heads down if they had to walk along the beach by his house.

"And then one evening, Captain Westcott rose slowly from his old rocking chair and hobbled to the water's edge. A few folks saw him, standing on the beach, his stooped shoulders braced against the wind. He stood there, still and silent, ignoring the rising tide as it licked at his shoes, then his calves, then his knees." Grannie Foster slowly walked her spindly fingers up Victoria's arm as she said this, raising goosebumps. "They watched him until his silhouette blended with the night. No one went after him, for fear of angering the sea. And that," Grannie Foster said, "was the last time anyone ever laid eyes on the old Captain with the house by the sea. He never returned to his creaky chair and no one ever found his body."

Grannie Foster was old herself and knew many things. And when she told Victoria that what the sea wants it keeps, Victoria knew what she said was true.

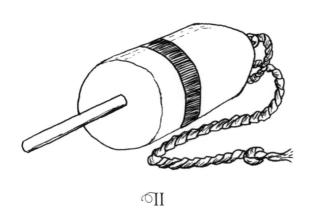

II

As she recalled the story, Victoria looked along the left bank of the cove and considered the Captain's rundown house. No one lived there. Years ago, when she was very young, a family had moved in and fixed the place up a bit. They left after a short time, though, and it had been empty since. The "For Sale" sign was split and hung haphazardly on its spike on the porch; it swung back and forth in the breeze, creaking like the Captain's chair. She turned her gaze out to the water, where ramshackle fishing boats dipped in the gentle swells of the outgoing tide. With the glow of morning behind them, their silhouettes danced before the wall of fog as if giant hands were playing at shadow puppets. Victoria watched the moored boats for a moment and then followed the line of shore along the right side of the cove. Halfway up the spit of pine, there was a path through the trees. It was narrow and dark, alive with mosquitoes and lined with thorny raspberry and blackberry bushes. She walked into the shelter of trees, and the predawn light barely touched her through their branches.

On the other side of the woods, the dirt track opened to another little cove with permanent pools of water and giant boulders perfect for climbing and sunbathing. There was lupine there too, huge swathes of purple and pink interspersed with swamp grass and cattail. The path continued down a muddy incline that filled with seawater at high tide. Around a bend in the shore, the fragile sand bar led to a soft, white beach with a border of driftwood and lupine. This was Victoria's place. This was where she painted.

Victoria never showed anyone her artwork. Her mother bought her canvases, sketchbooks, and paint when she asked for it, though never without a sigh or a grumble about her daughter's frivolous hobby. Often, Victoria's mother complained to Grannie Foster about Victoria's zeal for painting, her violent need for privacy. She didn't understand why Victoria persisted in walking along the dirty muddy beach at all hours of the day and night, why she didn't have friends or playmates.

"Now Maggie," Grannie Foster admonished. "All young girls have secrets. Even from their mothers." She nodded and winked at her daughter's narrowed eyes. "Her passion is the sea, and that is a passion too strong for you to fight. You know that. You'd do well to make your peace with it this time." Then a wry smile wended its way through the leathery wrinkles of her face and she continued on a laugh, "Who knows? Maybe we'll have a famous painter in the family someday."

But Maggie threw down the dishcloth and rounded on her mother, "Yes, I do know she loves the sea. That's all well and good. But don't you think these obsessions with the ocean have cost us enough already?" Her face darkened. "She could be up to anything down there by the shore, and I would never find out."

"Dear heart," Grannie replied, soothingly, "not to worry. It's just that she's an artist. It's what she loves. D'you know what she told me? That when she grows up, she wants to live in a house on the cove and paint it like a sunrise inside. So even when she's old and weak and can't go out, she'll have the ocean with her. Such beautiful dreams she has!" In response, Maggie snorted and lifted her rag to clean the kitchen counter once more.

Grannie Foster leveled an icy blue look on her daughter. "Maggie, the sea is her first love, and yes, that scares you! But don't you see? It is so much less complicated than it could be. You of all people should know that!"

So Victoria's mother relented. She let Victoria use the spare room as a studio, so the paint splatters and mess would be confined to one space. She gave Victoria a small brass key and promised never to enter unless invited, though she tempered this vow, saying she hoped Victoria would choose to share the paintings with her one day since she was paying for them. Victoria's studio door remained locked. It had one window that overlooked the hill leading to the cove. She spent hours there painting when she wasn't down by the shore.

III

The morning the sea took her, Victoria had hoped to capture on paper the last warmth of the fading summer. She had with her a sketchbook, a pencil, and a small set of watercolors. As she picked her way along the shore, the tide sucked away from the slimy stones and the sky glowed brighter through the low-lying fog. By the time she reached the large boulders on the other side of the forest path, dawn had broken. She scrambled up onto the largest boulder, where the view was clear with a perfect frame of green. As she drew, the tide ebbed and the fog burned away, first to mist, then to wisps of cloud across the pastel patchwork of the sky. Seagulls flew above and sandpipers pecked at the sand along the beach. When the sun had burned its warmth through the fog, she shed her sundress, revealing a baggy, worn bathing suit, and fished the towel from her bag. It was a tradition. The last day of summer, before school held her chained for another year, she always went for a swim out past the point and sunbathed on a small rocky island looking back at the shore.

The water was rougher than usual that day, but Victoria was a strong swimmer. She waded into the swirling surf and danced out until she was up to her waist. The cold water raised goosebumps but she persevered, kicking out with her legs and pulling fiercely with her arms in the direction of the point. When she had almost reached the rocky island, she flipped and floated on her back, letting the warmth of the August sun seep into her chilled skin. The exercise had warmed her, but the nip of imminent fall held on, slowing her down and starting a fine shiver from head to foot. She gave the sun another moment and then started for the island once more.

Without warning, an errant wave surged around a boulder at the edge of the island. With her head turned to the side, Victoria didn't see it crest in a frothy white mass above her. Suddenly she was caught. The wave sucked her down so fast she didn't have time to breathe. Her eyes were open, stinging and blurry with salt and sand. The water roiled in a fury around her; it bared its foamy teeth, as if it wanted to swallow her whole, and shook her until she didn't know if she was up or down. After a few moments spent battling vainly for a breath, Victoria let the hungry current have its way. She tossed and swirled through the sea's bubbling maw, arms and legs floating like pale eels around her, twisting like dead things. Her lungs burned.

Seaweed tangled in her hair as it flowed forward in the undertow and wrapped itself around her face. She watched her white fingers moving gracefully, aimlessly through the water and willed them to save her, willed them to find a way out. They just curled and uncurled gently in the current, like the sinuous tentacles of a sea anemone, and did nothing. Blinking, she struggled to hold onto the vision of her reaching hands, but the pale skin faded and the churning water turned into a cloud of darkness before her. She gave a last half-hearted kick.

What the sea wants it takes, she thought. And the sea wanted her.

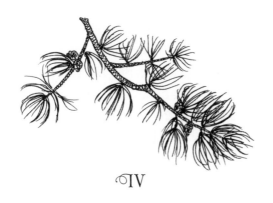

IV

Busy exploring the mossy, brambly forest, Sam didn't realize anything was wrong until he heard Dart barking down at the beach. It wasn't Dart's hyper "chasing birds" bark, or his "throw me a stick" bark. The small white and brown-splotched dog was howling like he meant to wake the dead. Sam ran, dark red juice dripping from the crushed raspberries in his hand. The speckled sunlight through the trees played tricks with his eyes and he paused for a moment when he reached the beach to let them adjust. Dropping the fruit, he wiped his wet, red hand on his trousers. The juice seeped into the fabric like blood, but Sam didn't notice. He could see Dart leaping in the air on the shore, dodging at the sea with singular purpose, then throwing himself back as the water foamed toward him. Sam looked at the water and suddenly saw what Dart saw. Floating in the insistent give and take of the waves was a body.

Sam sprinted to the beach and waded into the choppy water. The sea sucked at him, gnawing at his clothing and weighing down his shoes. He fought with all his strength to heave the limp weight of the girl from the grasping water. Finally, panting, he reached the safety of the beach, the body safely held in his arms.

The girl's skin was the pale bluish white of skimmed milk and her arms hung from their sockets like those of a rag doll. As gently as he could, he laid her down on her back on a dry patch of sand. Wildly, desperately, his eyes darted along the beach, the edge of the woods, down along the path to the cove, praying someone older and wiser would come to his rescue. No one in sight. He yelled, "Help! Help!" as loud as he could and Dart kept barking, jumping and pawing at the girl's arm. Sam closed his eyes. There wasn't time to be a coward. Dark shadows sat in the contours of her face and her lips were grayish blue.

He brushed her matted hair off her forehead and made sure her nose and mouth were clear. Taking a deep breath, he leaned over her still body and pushed straight down on her chest with his arms, three times. He paused, then continued the pattern. He kept brushing her hair back, whispering the same mantra over and over. "Breathe. Breathe. Breathe. Breathe." The rhythm formed a steady heartbeat in his head as he pushed against her chest.

It wasn't working. "Help! Please, someone help!" In the distance he thought he heard a shout. He forced her chest to compress three times more and his arms shook with the effort. This time he tried breathing into her mouth. It felt like hours since he'd pulled her from the water, though he knew it was only a minute or two.

Suddenly his mouth was full of salty water and he was coughing and she was coughing and foreheads were bumping and the girl was turning on her side and vomiting water into the sand. Sam slumped backwards and stared at the sky. He could hear her retching but all he could see was one impossibly white cloud, saucer shaped, surrounded by an infinite halo of blue. And then his view was obstructed by a furry head and madly licking tongue.

"Dart! Stop it!" he said, sitting up too quickly and knocking the dog's head with his own. He rubbed his forehead and gave Dart a hug. He looked over at the girl and saw that she was sitting with her head between her knees, arms curled around her legs, breathing heavy. He reached out a hand to touch her shoulder but stopped short, unsure. She turned, and the fierce look in her blue eyes sent a shiver along his scalp.

It took him a second to realize she was Victoria, the quiet girl who lived up the road. The blue lips and wild hair had changed her features, had made her look like someone, or something, else. "Oh. It's you," he said, suddenly shy. "Victoria." They'd never really spoken. He hadn't lived in the area for long. "Are—are you okay? What happened?"

Victoria stared at Sam. There were hazy sparkles in her eyes, making the sun too bright and blurry. It bleached out Sam's tan skin and sandy hair, as if he were nothing more than an overexposed photograph, an incomplete, two-dimensional representation of a thing. She blinked, and the world almost came back into focus. "I—I thought. I thought the sea had taken me," she said, shaking her head and sending sandy drops of water at Sam and Dart, who whimpered and danced out of range. "I, well I don't know what happened. I think...I thought—" Just then the distant shouting burst upon them and several adults raced along the beach. Sam's granddad was there along with a couple of fisherman from the cove. Suddenly there were arms grabbing Victoria and faces close to Sam's, asking him questions he couldn't follow in all the noise and movement. He thought he felt a familiar hand on his shoulder but he couldn't be sure. In all the confusion, Sam got pushed further and further from Victoria, but he kept watching her, and her eyes never left his face.

Later, just before falling asleep, Sam saw her again in his mind: her purplish blue lips, her pale, shadowed skin, her dark hair wrapping her face like rope. Then, in his almost dream, she opened her vivid blue eyes and stared, right down into his soul. He whispered her words to himself in the dark, "I thought the sea had taken me," and wondered why there hadn't been relief in her voice, only sadness. Almost, though he couldn't imagine why, she had sounded disappointed.

V

For many days, Victoria burned in bed with a fever. It gripped her so hard that every breath hurt, and she lay, silent and still, wrapped in clammy sheets. Grannie Foster sat with her day and night. She held her granddaughter's hand, stroked her forehead, and kept the damp and twisted hair out of her face. She watched every shallow breath and listened to every rasping cough. Victoria's mother paced outside the door and badgered the doctor with questions he couldn't answer. Sam stopped by one day, but he wasn't allowed to see the patient.

Victoria's mother answered Sam's uncertain knock. She stood in the doorway, her hand so tight on the jamb that her knuckles looked as though they'd push through her skin. "My dear boy, we can't thank you enough," she said. Her gaunt cheeks pulled her lips into a smile. "But right now is not a good time. My daughter is sick." The woman turned away from the door and walked into the house. Sam wasn't sure whether to follow; she left the door open but didn't invite him in. The entrance led to a large open kitchen and Sam watched as Mrs. Winslow fiddled at the kitchen sink. He was about to leave, when suddenly she threw down the rag she was wiping the counter with and turned on him.

"Such a silly thing to do, swimming this time of year. What could she have been thinking?" she ranted. Her face was red and her hands clenched and unclenched. He shrugged and looked down. "All the time, she has to be down by the water. Just like her father. I don't understand it. I never understood him, and I will never understand her! And now she may have killed herself with it—silly, stupid girl!" At these last words Mrs. Winslow's voice cracked and, to Sam's supreme discomfort, she started to sob. Before he could think of something comforting to say, or anything at all, she'd whirled around and started scrubbing the sink again. She scoured it, the muscles in her thin arms defined and quivering with the effort.

Sam stood in the doorway. What could he say? He cleared his throat, but the woman didn't turn around. "Well. Please let her know I was here. Oh, I picked these for her." He started forward to hand her the bundle of asters and coneflowers, but she didn't move to take them. So he walked to the kitchen counter and set them down, carefully avoiding the spot Victoria's mother was savagely cleaning. He paused, but she just whispered, "That damn

sea," and so Sam left. He wondered if he would ever see Victoria again.

Victoria might have died then. But one night, as Grannie Foster found herself slipping into sleep at her post by her granddaughter's bed, Victoria's fever broke with no commotion at all. The first thing Victoria saw when she opened her eyes was her mother's face. Mrs. Winslow laid her hand against Victoria's cheek and then she stood back and glared. "You irresponsible child. How could you worry us like that? What were you thinking?" Grannie Foster sat in her rocking chair and patted Victoria's hand. Victoria said nothing and ignored her mother; she just stared into Grannie Foster's eyes. They were sky blue and weighed down by wrinkles, and they didn't blink or falter.

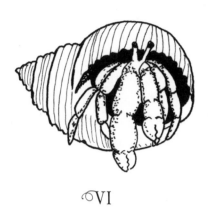

VI

It wasn't until early October that Victoria was strong enough to leave her house and walk down to the beach. And even then, she didn't hurry to the shore each dawn with the joy she'd once shown. She didn't take her art kit. She didn't cross the wooded path to the little sandy beach.

Sam saw her sometimes when he was out playing with Dart. He'd watch her sitting at the edge of the trees, staring at the water, not moving. She always looked so small and alone, with the great shadows of the forest behind her.

One day he decided to speak to her. He walked to the edge of the road, where it dead-ended at the cove, and picked his way across the rocks to where she was sitting. Dart was distracted by the scent of field mice in the marshy grass at the edge of the wood and didn't follow. The tide was half out, but the line of dried seaweed and broken shells it left behind was just at Victoria's feet. She was sitting as he remembered her from that August day, knees pulled up, arms wrapped around them. A sinuous piece of seaweed curled along the top of her shoe and he wondered if it was actually possible that she'd been sitting there, not moving, since high tide. It was cold and she was huddled into her overcoat, her head protected by a red woolen cap.

"Hi," he said softly, lowering himself to the sandy grass. "How are you doing? Do you remember me?"

Victoria turned and looked at Sam. He wasn't wearing a hat and his fair hair needed a cut. It curled wildly around his thin face and he had to keep brushing it out of his eyes. His cheeks were red and rough from the wind. "Hi Sam," she said, and he looked away, staring out at the sea, nervous suddenly. Her quiet voice continued, "I come here a lot. I guess you know—I see you sometimes with your dog on the beach down there." She pointed vaguely to the right, where the shore curved around, cupping its little bit of sea. In the distance they could see Dart huffling in the bushes and darting erratically in pursuit of some delicious scent.

"Are—really, are you okay?" he asked, risking a quick glance at her.

Victoria sighed. She squinted into the sun for a moment and then returned Sam's look. "You know, Grannie Foster once told me something about the sea. She said that it has a soul, like you and me, and that the sea weeps and laughs and screams, just like we do. She said, 'The sea's

soul wants things, takes things. It'll cradle dying sailors in its watery arms, and it'll spit out murdered bodies, just so people know a sin took place.' Grannie Foster told me that the sea's alive, that it sees things, and it feels things too." Victoria's eyes bored into Sam's. "What do you think?" she asked, breaking eye contact at last. "Do you think that's crazy?" She looked down between her knees and pushed a broken shell around in the sand.

He watched her for a moment, then shifted his gaze out to the water. It was a cold day but a bright one, and the sun fluttered against the swells like millions of diamonds. "I think the sea is laughing today," he said, and then he cringed, realizing how stupid he sounded. But the impossibly pale, dark-haired girl beside him glanced up, and she laughed. Her face didn't look fierce anymore. Sam shrugged and gave a half-hearted laugh in return. Suddenly she grabbed his arm and pulled him to his feet, and then they were slipping and sliding down the wet rocks to the edge of the water, skipping stones and playing. They ran along the beach, and Sam called Dart, and the three of them frolicked by the water until long purple strokes of light lit the sky behind them and spread across the blue, burning the cloud edges with red and turning the water pink. And that night, for the first time since the accident, Victoria dreamt of the sea.

The next morning, Victoria asked her mother for paint and canvas. The older woman complied, lips pursed when

Victoria made her request. She had hoped her daughter was looking to other things.

It didn't take long before Victoria's hands were stained and splotched with paint. She stared out the windows down to the shore and forgot little things, like clearing the table or cleaning out the sink—things that had been habit for years.

Rocking slowly in her chair in the living room, Grannie Foster closed her eyes when Victoria's mother nagged. The old woman rocked and rocked and watched her granddaughter with heavy-lidded eyes; it was as if a pale little ghost with tangled dark hair had come to live with them, and Grannie Foster didn't know how to give the spirit peace. Victoria's walks to the shore got longer and longer and she'd come home breathless and shaking with cold. Often she would return after dusk, and her mother would squeeze her lips into a tight, thin line and clean the kitchen viciously, saying nothing. Victoria didn't spend hours in her studio like she once did; she spent little time in the house at all, but she never stopped asking for art supplies.

Grannie Foster tried to talk to Victoria, but she wasn't interested in her grandmother's stories anymore, not even the ones about the sea.

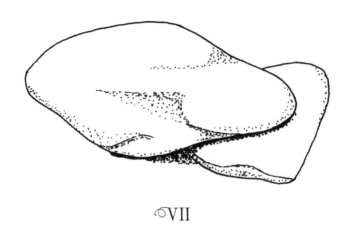

VII

After the day at the beach, when Victoria had grabbed his arm and let him teach her how to skip stones, Sam hadn't seen Victoria, at least not up close. Occasionally he watched her walk along the beach, but she was always far away, and if she saw him she gave no sign. With the cold weather and snow of winter upon the little town, Sam spent more time indoors, curled up with a book by the fire, Dart snoring softly in his lap. The sea held no power over him. It was something cold and distant now, something patiently waiting for him and the summer to return.

One morning, as he walked down the beach to the road, he saw Victoria steal furtively along the cove. He was meant to be walking to school, and so was she. But instead she headed away from the road, toward the Captain's cabin. Sam stared at her, and then turned and considered the snow-dusted lane. It stretched up through the pines away from him, twisting into shadow. He was late anyway. He turned and followed the line of pine trees around the cove, trying to blend in. He didn't know why he was hiding from Victoria, except that it was obvious she herself didn't want to be seen.

The weather had been wild all week, and this morning was no different. Clouds crowded the sky, their heavy gray weight sinking low enough to touch the mist that hovered out to sea. Snowflakes swirled around Sam as he made his way across the crunchy ground to the rundown cottage. Just as he reached the house, he slipped and fell to his knees. When his kneecaps hit cold unyielding rock he bit his lip and grunted. Gingerly he got his feet under him, wriggling his legs through the pain. He was going to have some good bruises from that one. He carried on, taking extra care with his footing until he reached the house. Having lost its battle against the insistent ocean wind, the "For Sale" sign lay despondent on the rocky shore under the stilts that held up the front porch. Here, the beach was narrow, so that the rear of the house backed up against the woods. Bushes had grown up along the side of the cabin with no one to trim them back.

Sam had been inside the house once, when he and his granddad were thinking of moving to the area, but it had been in such disrepair they hadn't considered it an option for long. He sidled up to the window of the front room and peered through the dirty glass. The room was empty save for an overturned, dilapidated wooden chair. Wallpaper peeled from the walls like strips of skin and a mouse skittered unconcernedly across the floor, dodging dust bunnies and leaves that had blown in through a broken window on the other side of the room. No Victoria. The back room and kitchen were also empty. That left the loft, a big open room above the porch with wide windows and a view of the ocean.

Sam hunched into his jacket as the snow intensified. It swirled around him, smelling of salt and fish. He liked the clean snows better, the ones that swept down from inland—they smelled like fir tips and wood smoke. He walked around to the back door and saw it had been left ajar. As quietly as he could, he pushed into the house. Just in front of him was the staircase. It still looked as it had a couple of years ago, solid but ugly, covered in stained, ragged carpet. It was the weather that did it, blowing in with its damp and chill, the salt air sanding off paint and wallpaper, ruining carpet and hardwood floors.

Watching his feet as he climbed the stairs, Sam tested each step for soundness, hoping it wouldn't creak. He didn't want to scare Victoria. He would wait until he could see her before announcing himself, so she'd know he wasn't some stranger, up to no good.

He had almost reached the top step when a noise above made him raise his head. Before he knew what was happening, a small, sturdy mass hurtled at him and he went tumbling down the stairs, carrying someone, or something, with him. As soon as he came to rest at the bottom of the stairs, he crawled backward, ignoring the pain in his wrists and knees, terrified of the writhing specter before him. All he could see was wild hair and flowing black cloth, wraithlike in the dim light of the hall. He realized they were both yelling, his "Help! Help!" and her "Get out! Get out!" sounding strangely dissonant, like the cawing of two seagulls fighting over clams in the bay.

Finally, breathlessly, his senses returned and he realized it was only Victoria. Again, he hadn't recognized her, so different had her appearance become. The wild dark hair hid her face and eyes and her figure, swathed in a black garment, looked strange and misshapen.

"Stop! Stop, Victoria!" he yelled to get her attention. "It's just me, Sam!"

Her voice kept up its resolute harping. "Get out! Get out, Sam! Get out!" She grabbed him by the arms and pushed him until he fell backwards through the door into sandy brush. She stood over him, looking down with the snow alighting on her hair, stark and white against the black. He could see her eyes now, and they were flashing.

"God, Victoria. What's wrong?" He stared up at her and shivered.

"Sorry, Sam. You can't come in," she said, her voice hard. "Not yet. Maybe not ever." She paused, and for a moment her eyes softened. "I'm sorry if I scared you." She turned to go into the house.

"Wait! What do you mean?" Recovering his wits, Sam felt his face flush with anger as his voice rose. "You know, you could have killed me just now. Broken my neck on those stairs. Or killed yourself! What is your problem?"

He scrambled to his feet. He was shaky and there were points of pain all over his body from the knocks and twists he took going down the stairs.

Victoria stopped with her back to him, her shoulders hunched. The black cloth swirled around her in the wind. When Sam finished, there was a moment of silence, and he watched her splotchy black dress move and the way the snow fell all around her. "Sorry," she said again. She turned back for a moment and looked at him over her shoulder. He shifted his feet and rubbed a sore spot on his elbow, anger diffused by her strange expression.

"What are you wearing?" he asked, not sure what else to say and awkward with the silence.

Suddenly her smile broke through, a beam of light piercing a morning mist. "Oh," she laughed, "this is just my painting dress. I put it over my clothes so they don't get dirty." For a moment she was the skipping stones Victoria again. She giggled and bobbed a jaunty curtsy on the stair.

"You paint? That's neat!" he replied with enthusiasm. She bent her head and a blush swept across her pale cheeks.

"You think so?" she asked shyly.

"Of course! What kinds of things do you paint?"
And suddenly the switch flipped. Victoria drew back across the doorway, her black hair and dress speckled with paint and snow.

"See you around, Sam," she said, as she disappeared inside the shadows of the house.

VIII

Sam lived with his granddad in an old salt-box house on Victoria's lane. It was nestled in the woods close to the water, hidden from the road and beach by immense pine trees. Sam's parents had died when he was very young and his earliest memories were filled with the spicy, musky scent of his grandfather's pipe. The old man was energetic for his age and he took care of his grandson with a gentle absentmindedness that suited Sam just fine.

Sitting by the fire that night, snow swirling outside the windows under the porch light, Sam found he couldn't concentrate on his book.

"Granddad, do you like it here?" he asked, staring into the slowly curling flames of the fire.

His grandfather looked up from his newspaper. "Sure. It's peaceful, right by the water. It reminds me of where I grew up, near Bar Harbor." He looked at Sam's face, turned away and glowing red in the firelight. He folded the newspaper and set it on the table beside him. "Why, Sam? Do you like it here?"

"I suppose. I don't know."

"Hmm. Why is that?" His grandfather's voice was soft.

"It's not anything, really. It's just that—well, there's this girl who lives up the road. Victoria—"

"The girl you saved. I remember her." Sam tore his eyes from the fire and glanced at the older man. His grandfather winked. "Pretty."

Sam's face glowed more ferociously than the fire could account for and he turned away. "It's not like that. That's not what I meant." He cleared his throat. "I just wonder sometimes. She's not like anyone I know. She's sort of strange—says strange things. I saw her today and, well— she frightened me a little."

The old man cocked his craggy, gray-haired head to the side, considering Sam's words. "What about her frightened you?"

"I don't know, exactly. It was just the way she looked sort of, her eyes burning out of her face. And the way she talks about the sea like it's a person. She doesn't care about what other girls seem to care about. She's just—different."

His grandfather chuckled, "You're right! She sounds like an odd duck to me. But the odd ones aren't necessarily bad, you know." He settled back into his chair and picked up his pipe from the table. Sam knew this meant his grandfather was gearing up for a story.

"You know, when your father was your age," he began, as

he lit the pipe and took a few puffs, "he was a little strange too. He always talked about death. I think he frightened a lot of people. He questioned everything—himself, reality, what it meant to die. You know, what it felt like, that kind of thing. He wondered if Jesus was real and if there was an afterlife—talked about the strange rites of ancient cultures I'd never even heard of." At this Sam perked up and his granddad grinned. "Yes, all boys are interested in the macabre. But your father would make you think about those things as they pertained to you." Sam's granddad took a couple of thoughtful puffs on his pipe and they both watched the fragrant smoke curl up on a current of air. "Honestly? It frightened me a little, how morbid he was. I didn't know how to talk to him, how to get him to enjoy life more. But he was a nice kid and my son so I listened to him, when I could stand it." He smiled wryly and Sam grinned back.

"That's right, Sam. I'm not saying it's easy with the strange ones! But you know what?" Sam's grandfather's eyes shifted to the fire and lost their focus. "I can still remember a lot of our conversations—we really tried to work things out so that it all made sense." His voice grew quiet. "And it was rough going sometimes but I'll tell you, some of the things we talked about then comfort me to this day." He paused, and a warm silence settled on the room.

Then Sam's granddad smiled, shook his head, and patted Sam's hand. "Especially when I think about your father. He was a brave man, and he wasn't scared of death. He knew he had a good life when he had you." Sam smiled.

And so, when Sam saw Victoria on the beach, he sought her out. Sometimes she'd see him and wave him away, disappearing into the Captain's cabin. He'd find himself staring after her, annoyed that she wouldn't share her secrets with him. Every now and then, she'd knock on his back door and they would take Dart down to the shore and make snow angels on the beach. Those were the good times. Sam didn't ask what she did in the Captain's house, in spite of his desperate curiosity. He knew it would just make her clam up further. So he begged her to tell him stories about the sea, and she obliged magnificently. He would lose himself in her tales of sailors and pirates and the beautiful women who waited for them to return from their travels at sea. The way she told the tales he could almost believe it himself, that the sea was as living and breathing a thing as any human. Best of all, he liked the rare occasions when she'd accept his offer of hot cocoa on a cold afternoon, when they'd flash smiles beneath chocolate milk moustaches at each other.

Sam tried to take his granddad's advice and stick with Victoria, but it was never very long before her face would darken and she'd slip away again, leaving Sam to wander the shore alone, hurling stones into the unheeding water.

Maggie Winslow had her own concerns about Victoria. Some days—the days spent with her new friend Sam—Victoria galloped through the house, blissfully happy. Most days, however, the girl held a darkness around her that Maggie could not understand. Grannie Foster's reassurances fell into silence, as she rocked endlessly in her chair. It was as if Victoria were a punctured hot air balloon, spinning wildly out of control, and all the women could do was watch helplessly as she fell. There were graceful moments when she floated lightly on a breeze, and others when she spiraled straight down into the black.

At the end of November, Victoria stopped going to school altogether. Her teachers made visits to the house, entreated Maggie to make her daughter toe the line. Maggie thought about denying her daughter art supplies, walking her to school each day, but the stare Victoria gave her when she threatened these things deterred her. The girl's face would go pale and her eyes would burn; somehow, Victoria would find a way.

IX

Deep in winter, very near midnight on Christmas Eve, a tapping woke Sam. His bedroom door was ajar, and a glow from the Christmas tree lights in the living room permeated the dark. The sound started again, a light tapping on his window. Groggy with sleep he turned toward the noise and opened bleary eyes. He found himself staring out the window into a pale, disembodied face, floating in the dim glow of the moon. He yelled and fell backward off his bed with a thud. His grandfather's eeriest ghost stories came back to him in a flash. Slowly he crawled to his knees, tangled in the sheets, and prayed the face would be gone from the window, wondering what spirit had chosen to visit him.

When he finally steeled himself to look again, the face was still there, framed in darkness. A hand tapped on the window next to the face. He blinked. It was Victoria. She was mouthing his name and beckoning to him. Sam felt the fear lessen, only slightly. The look in her eyes was unlike anything he'd ever seen. He wasn't sure, even then, that she wasn't a ghost.

He tiptoed out of his room, grabbing his winter coat and boots on the way. Dart remained curled at the bottom of the bed, nose tucked under a paw. Sam glanced at him as he left, surprised the little spitfire wasn't doing his guard dog act. His granddad didn't seem to have awakened either. Victoria waited at the back door.

Grabbing his arm, she led him into the deeper darkness of the woods behind the house, where the Christmas lights didn't reach. The night was bitterly cold and clear, and clean shafts of moonlight speared through the trees around them.

"Sam, Sam, I'm finished," she whispered, holding onto his arm as if she couldn't stand without it.

"Finished what? Victoria, what are you doing out this late? What's going on?" Sam could barely see her, just a pale slash where her face should have been, partially touched by moonlight. He almost thought he could see her eyes, glowing like a cat's, but he knew that was nothing but his imagination. Already, he was shaking with cold.

"Oh, Sam. My paintings. I finished them. I can go now. I know I can. I know it'll let me go." Victoria's voice was breathy and light and she laughed giddily and did a little spin in the moonlight, arms wide. She stumbled and grabbed at his shoulders to keep from falling, giggles escaping her like bubbles.

"What are you talking about? Lord in heaven, Victoria.

50

It's freezing out here! And it's the middle of the night. Really, can't you for once just be a normal friend and do normal things?"

Victoria pushed back from him and stood under her own power. The white shape of her face stared into his.

"Sam—"

"Look, I'm sorry. It's just that I'm cold and tired and I wasn't expecting to see you, staring in at me through my window. I thought you were a ghost! The cryptic talk isn't helping my mood either. You're cold. I'm cold. Let's go inside and we can talk properly."

"No, Sam. I'm not going inside. I just came to say goodbye."

He tried to reply but she went on, covering his mouth with her hand.

"You saved me. That day in the sea. And you were my friend. I never thanked you for that. For any of it." She paused. "I am truly sorry, Sam. I know you don't understand me. But you were my friend anyway, and I will always be grateful for that."

And then she kissed him. Sam was still trying to rein in his frustration when he felt her chilled lips on his. It was the last thing he expected and, caught by the strangeness of it all, he didn't react immediately, just felt with a new kind of intrigue the soft coldness of her lips and the warmth of her breath in contrast.

And then, just as suddenly, she was gone. He listened for noise of her making her way through the woods but could hear nothing over the icy groan of the wind. He called her name, over and over, and circled in the darkness, searching for some hint of her presence. Nothing. His anger and confusion melted away. What had she meant she was saying goodbye? The town church bells rang, the sound carrying over the currents of breeze. Midnight. Christmas Day. Many long minutes after the bells faded into the whistle of the wind, Sam stood there, twisting in the darkness. He didn't know what to do. As he waited for some sign of her, the cold seeped through the thin flannel of his pajamas and slid insidiously up under his coat. He called her name again, staring vainly into the darkness. Then he made his way back inside, stumbling as he followed the dim glow of the still-lit Christmas tree.

When he entered the house, he immediately smelled pipe smoke. His granddad was sitting in one of the leather chairs by the cold fireplace, Dart in his lap, framed by the blinking red and green lights of the tree. Sam walked toward him, not knowing what to say.

"Nice night for a walk," Sam's grandfather said, taking several short puffs on his pipe. "You all right?"

"Granddad, I saw her. Victoria. She said she wanted to thank me for being her friend. She wanted to say goodbye. She—she was acting so strange!" Sam found he was shaking still, though he couldn't tell if it was from the cold or something else. His granddad sat up and put his pipe in the ashtray on the coffee table.

"Well, that doesn't sound good." He frowned. "It's late,

but it seems to me we should give the Winslows a call." He crossed to the phone and dialed the operator. Sam paced as his grandfather murmured softly into the phone. There was a pause and then, "Thank you. Sorry to bother you. Goodnight. And Merry Christmas." The older man gently replaced the phone in the hanger and turned to his grandson.

"Well, I wonder if maybe the holidays are getting to you more than usual this year." Confused, Sam turned to him and stopped his pacing. "Mrs. Winslow just checked on Victoria. She's asleep in bed. Maggie didn't want to wake her, but she saw her sure enough. So, unless Victoria ran up the hill and snuck into her bed in the few minutes you were outside, I'd say you were having a bad dream and sleepwalking." He crossed the room and squeezed Sam's shoulder. "It's all right, Sam. She's safe in bed."

Sam went to bed himself, uneasy, and stared at his ceiling until morning. He didn't go to sleep. He was afraid he would dream.

X

The next day, as soon as his granddad released him from his gift-opening duties, Sam ran up the hill to Victoria's house. Dart followed him, his nails clicking a steady tattoo on the shells that covered the dirt road to keep it from eroding. When Sam reached the house, he knocked on the door and waited, shifting from foot to foot as his breathing calmed. No one answered. Knocking again, he peered through the window next to the door. The shades were drawn but he could just catch a glimpse through a break in the fabric. And he saw—nothing.

He ran to the front of the house along the porch and pressed his whole body against the French doors, cupping his hands around his face to keep out the glare. Again, nothing. No furniture, no pictures on the wall, no throw rugs. The house was completely empty. It wasn't just Victoria. Grannie Foster, Mrs. Winslow—the whole family had disappeared.

Sam wandered around the house, peering into every window. Every room looked like the next, empty save for light glitterings of dust hanging in the narrow beams of sun that slipped through drawn curtains. He stood with his hands on the porch railing and ignored the twinges of pain as his fingers curled around rose and raspberry thorns. He looked down toward the sea. The day was bright and cold, and the fog stayed offshore, barely visible past the furthest point of the cove. Small sweeps of cloud floated through the blue of the sky. The meadow was mostly covered with snow, but there were patches where animals had kicked up dirt and crusty, ice-tipped meadow grass. Dart was out front exploring the field, only his short straight tail and the brown splotch on his back visible in the snow. Sam looked around and dug his hands into the shriveled twinings of vine along the railing, disbelieving. As his glance passed along the garden out past the house, a dark shadow caught his eye. He turned and walked toward the shadow. Just as he reached the edge of the porch, Dart raced across the meadow and stood before him, ears and tail at attention. He barked madly at the thing in the garden.

There, hanging above the snowy hillocks of sleeping vegetables, shifting slightly in the breeze, was a scarecrow. It had no head; it was just a mass of dark and splotchy cloth tacked to a post in the middle of what, in summer, was the lettuce patch. Victoria's painting smock. Its billowing arms fluttered and fell, reaching out to him, a shroud empty and limp without its body. Dart barked and barked. Sam turned

away and ran, the image of the black dress chasing him all the way down the hill.

Rumors rampaged through the small community. No one had known the Winslows were moving; no one knew where they went. One neighbor thought maybe they'd gone to live with Maggie's brother-in-law, down the coast. Someone suggested maybe they'd moved inland. It was no secret that Mrs. Winslow hated the seaside. There was even conjecture that old Grannie Foster had died and Maggie was no longer tied to a place that held such painful memories. The rumors about Victoria were quieter, darker. There had been whispers ever since the day she'd been saved from the sea. Ancient superstitions were retold. The old sailors wondered.

"First her daddy gets taken," they said, "then she goes in and the sea wants her too. But the boy intervened and Victoria lived. That isn't the way of things." They shook their heads and their frowns were more nervous than sad. And no one would say it but the oldest ones wondered whether Victoria had paid her debt to the sea.

Sam didn't hear the rumors. He didn't wonder or worry what people were saying, what answers they had for the Winslows' disappearance. Victoria was gone. And she had never explained anything to him. He spent long hours walking the beach with Dart, staring at the Captain's house. What had she been doing there? What secrets were hidden in that house? Sam replayed every conversation they'd had, every story she'd told him. He sat in silence in the evenings, staring at the fire, remembering Victoria's eyes when she talked about the sea, wondering what it was that made them burn so. His grandfather's worried looks and well-meaning questions went unnoticed and unanswered. Each day Sam watched the sucking heartbeat of the surf, until he felt it under his skin and found that he carried the rhythm within him. And then he thought of Victoria's painting, and he longed to know what she had discovered in that strange little house, what answer she'd found to the inexorable pull of the sea. But the memory of her flying down the stairs, a violent specter in the shadows of the hall, kept him at bay. And so he walked the beach, wondering, waiting for some sign that her secrets were now his to know.

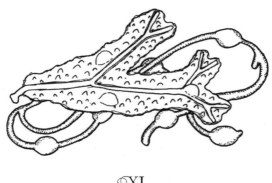

XI

The day the sea took Sam, dawn broke bright and mild and there was no fog. It was the first day that didn't smell of winter and Sam woke, refreshed and free, for once, of thoughts of Victoria. Dart sat dejectedly by the back door as Sam, whistling, left for school.

Just as he reached the crest of the hill, keeping his eyes away from Victoria's house as he passed, a movement at the edge of the wood startled him. He glanced toward the flash and saw, to his bemusement, a tiny black kitten, rolling in the grass along the road. The animal was so small she looked like nothing more than a dusty fluff of fur, with two pointed ears the only indication of her true identity. Slowly Sam approached, not wanting to scare her.

"Hey there, little bit," he whispered, crouching down to her level. "What are you doing here?" The kitten stopped, mid-roll, and stared at him upside down, her tummy bared. He reached out a tentative hand. Suddenly, she yowled as if in pain and skittered down the road toward the water, mewing pitifully. Sam followed, worried that she was injured or lost.

He gave her distance, so as not to frighten her more, and by the time he reached the beach she was out of sight. The water was gentle that day, so he could hear her soft cries above the sound of the waves. Following the noise, he called to her. Gradually the sound faded, and Sam found himself, inevitably, standing before the Captain's cabin.

He circled the old cabin twice, looking into windows, staring in at the strips of blistering wallpaper. He brushed a hand along the rough clapboard walls. Thoughts rocketed through his head and his heart pounded in his throat. At last he made his way into the house and slowly climbed the steps, watching the landing above him instead of his feet, his breath held, wondering what spirit would push him down the stairs this time.

He reached the landing safely and paused. Before him stood a sturdy oak door, blackened with age. The brass doorknob was tarnished, with a dark bit of rag stuffed into the keyhole. Without windows to let in the light, the landing was dim and it smelled faintly of mold. Sam held out a shaking hand to open the door. The wood had swelled in the damp, so he had to push with his hip to get it open, and he almost lost his nerve. He suddenly recalled the image of Victoria's bloodless, blue-pale face the day he pulled her from the sea. What price had she paid for

her survival?

The door gave and he stepped into the loft, just as a bright flash of morning light cascaded through the windows. Sam drew in a breath and gaped at the contents of the room. Victoria was there, breathing, staring out at him. In every stroke of paint, every color, every line, he saw her. For a moment the jumble of blues and pinks and vibrant greens dazzled his eyes and then specific images came into focus. To one side of the window several paintings leaned neatly against the wall. The picture on the top of the pile showed the cove on a calm, bright day. The sea was flat and blue, a vivid color matched by the sky. In the center of the image, sparkling with multicolored brilliance, a perfectly rendered mermaid tail caught the sunlight.

In another painting, a woman stood in silhouette on a cliff. A storm raged behind her and the ocean frothed below, clawing up the rock wall, desperately reaching for her. The tension in her figure and her billowing clothes and wild hair straining toward the sea caught Sam and he couldn't look away. He imagined that at any moment the wind would pull her to the edge and she would fall, eaten by the hungry water. He wanted to reach out and draw her back to safety. Finally, he tore his eyes from the painting and moved on. Some paintings were serene, depicting the cove as he knew it, swathed in lupine and cattail, seagulls floating on an almost visible breeze. Others showed scenes from Victoria's stories, with white-sailed ships floundering or flying jauntily below pirate flags.

As gently as he could, Sam moved the paintings around so he could study each one. Faster and faster he found himself flipping through the canvases, devouring each image with his eyes. He found a small painting of Dart, whom Victoria had depicted as a quivering mass of energy, leaping with a joyous lack of restraint at a thrown stick on the beach. Without a moment's thought, Sam reached for the painting and cradled it to his chest. He carried it with him while he explored the rest of the room, knowing even then that the picture would remain in this room, with the rest. Toward the bottom of a stack of paintings in the corner, he discovered one of himself. It was disconcerting, looking into his own thoughtful eyes. She'd painted him sitting on a boulder near where he'd saved her. He was staring out of the canvas, the sea to his back, his hands full of raspberries. They were spilling onto his lap from his hands and he was stained all over with raspberry blood.

Most of the images were barren of people. They were landscapes, images of the sea. The sea's character took the place of a human subject and, remembering Victoria's words on the beach so long ago, Sam found he could see in her paintings moments where the sea wept, laughed, screamed.

And more than that, all around him, the room itself was painted as a sunrise, the soft warm colors of dawn mixed with the dark splash of a coming storm. The walls were the cove, every line of the shore, of the trees, of the lupine that Victoria loved. Even the darkness, the power of the sea was there, in the storm clouds on the horizon, the whitecaps hovering off shore. Sam understood what she meant now, the disappointment in her voice when he'd saved her from the ocean. She had wanted to be taken. And she had found a way. She'd put it all there, given all of herself. The spirit of the sea mingled with Victoria's in the paintings, and Sam stood, drinking in the imagery. The sea had asked a steep price for her life after all and this was her payment, this shrine to the sea.

Hours later, Sam finally closed the door to the loft and walked thoughtfully down the stairs. As he left the house, he looked into the rundown living room, at the chair sitting broken and alone on the floor. And he thought that maybe someday he would fix that chair, fix it so he could sit and linger over Victoria's paintings in comfort.

As it happened, he did fix the chair. Victoria had said she was free, but the more he thought about it, the more he knew that couldn't be so. How could she be, when all of her was there, waiting in that room? He knew she would come back. And he would keep it safe, her house by the sea. He would keep it safe until she returned.

So Sam kept vigil over the house. He spent hours in the room of paintings. He followed the path of the sun with his eyes as the ever-changing light played on the colors of Victoria's creations. Every time he heard a sigh of breeze or creak of wood he turned, hopeful, praying it was Victoria's sigh, Victoria's foot on the stair.

Many years later, after his granddad had passed away, Sam bought the Captain's crumbling house. He fixed the chair in the rotting living room and placed it on the porch, and he rocked. He waited. And he watched the sea. He watched it through all the seasons and years of his life. After a long time, it occurred to him that Victoria was, indeed, free. The sea wanted him now. Perhaps it had wanted him all along.

And so the stories continued, about the old man by the sea. Children dared each other to touch the stilts that held up his porch and ran away, giggling, when they heard the thud of his chair above them. No one remembered his name. Villagers would hurry by his cabin, and the rocking of his chair would echo after them, regular as the heartbeat of the ocean.

There was a legend that lived in the town, long after the old man's chair creaked into silence. No one knew who told it first or how it came to be. Some said that long ago, when the man was young, he fell in love with a mermaid. Her tail glittered and winked at him on a bright summer's day as she dove in the sea and he swam after her, enchanted by her beauty. And so she left the sea for him, to live in his little cottage on the bay. After some time, the lovely mermaid missed her home. She painted the house as a sunrise, to bring the sea to her so she wouldn't miss it so. But she aged and weakened, without the water to feed her soul. One night a storm raged into the quiet little bay. The sea swept into the house in a fury and took back its daughter on a wave so large it swallowed the house whole. But the sea receded, leaving the house intact, for it did not want the man to follow.

Though no one has seen him in many years, people say he sits there still, rocking on his porch. They speak of how he waits, alone in his sunrise-painted house, for his love to return, or the day when the sea shows mercy and welcomes him at last.

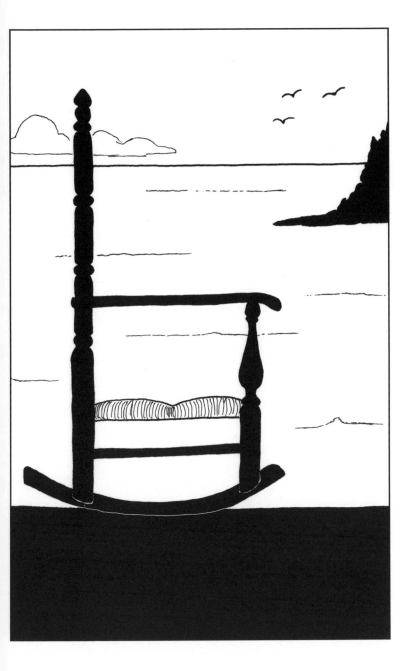

Acknowledgements

This project began as the thesis for my master's degree in Publishing from Oxford Brookes University. It has become so much more than that. The support and encouragement I've received from family, friends, and professors have made the experience the most worthy and transforming of my life. I couldn't have done it without all of you. There are a few people I would like to mention by name, for their special and much appreciated contributions to this book.

First of all, thank you to all my professors at Oxford Brookes University, especially Adrian Bullock and Jane Potter, for your wisdom, advice, and encouragement. To Richard Hart and Jane Parker, thank you for sharing your experiences with me in creating your own publishing house. Norman White, of Biddles, thank you for your patience, warmth, and professionalism. Many thanks to my fearless and discerning editors, especially Jackie McCosh, Julia Blum, Helen Duriez, Fatima Petersen, Laura Blum, Michael Blum, Marty, Ray, Suzanne, and Betty Banghart. Your insight, critique, support, and patience were invaluable. To Michael Blum, thank you for your guidance and all your hard work in support of the book. And in an 11th hour tour de force, thanks go out to Andy Chang; without you, well, what can I say?

Finally, to Julia, thank you for being the best friend and creative guide a girl could have.

71